Jimmy Takes Vanishing Lessons

Jimmy Takes Vanishing Lessons

by Walter R. Brooks

ILLUSTRATED BY DON BOLOGNESE

THE OVERLOOK PRESS

WOODSTOCK & NEW YORK

This edition first published in the United States in 2007 by
The Overlook Press, Peter Mayer Publishers, Inc.
Woodstock & New York

WOODSTOCK:
One Overlook Drive
Woodstock, NY 12498
www.overlookpress.com
[for individual orders, bulk and special sales, contact our Woodstock office]

NEW YORK:
141 Wooster Street
New York, NY 10012

Library of Congress Cataloging-in-Publication Data

Brooks, Walter Rollin, 1856–1958l
Jimmy takes vanishing lessons. Illustrated by Don Bolognese.
p. cm.

"First published in Story parade magazine."

1. Bolognese, Don, illus. I. Title
PZ7.B799rJi   65-21554

Printed in Singapore
ISBN-13 978-1-58567-895-2
10 9 8 7 6 5 4 3 2 1

Jimmy Takes Vanishing Lessons

*T*he school bus picked up Jimmy Crandall every morning at the side road that led up to his aunt's house, and every afternoon it dropped him there again. And so, twice a day, on the bus, he passed the entrance to the mysterious road.

It wasn't much of a road any more. It was choked with weeds and blackberry bushes, and the woods on both sides pressed in so closely that the branches met overhead, and it was dark and gloomy even on bright days. The bus driver once pointed it out.

"Folks that go in there after dark," he said, "well, they usually don't ever come out again. There's a haunted house about a quarter of a mile down that road." He paused. "But you ought to know about that, Jimmy. It was your grandfather's house."

Jimmy knew about it, and he knew that it now belonged to his Aunt Mary. But Jimmy's aunt would never talk to him about the house. She said the stories about it were silly nonsense, and there were no such things as ghosts. If all the villagers weren't a lot of superstitious idiots, she would be able to rent the house, and then she would have enough money to buy Jimmy some decent clothes and take him to the movies.

Jimmy thought it was all very well to say that there were no such things as ghosts, but how about the people who had tried to live there? Aunt Mary had rented the house three times, but every family had moved out within a week. They said the things that went on there were just too queer. So, nobody would live in it any more.

Jimmy thought about the house a lot. If he could only prove that there wasn't a ghost. . . .

And one Saturday, when his aunt was in the village, Jimmy took the key to the haunted house from its hook on the kitchen door, and started out.

It had seemed like a fine idea when he had first thought of it—to find out for himself. Even in the silence and damp gloom of the old road, it still seemed pretty good. Nothing to be scared of, he told himself. Ghosts aren't around in the daytime. But, when he came out in the clearing and looked at those blank, dusty windows, he wasn't so sure.

"Oh, come on!" he told himself. And he squared his shoulders and waded through the long grass to the porch.

Then he stopped again. His feet did not seem to want to go up the steps. It took him nearly five minutes to persuade them to move. But when at last they did, they marched right up and across the porch to the front door, and Jimmy set his teeth hard and put the key in the keyhole. It turned with a squeak. He pushed the door open and went in.

That was probably the bravest thing that Jimmy had ever done. He was in a long, dark hall with closed doors on both sides, and on the right, the stairs went up. He had left the door open behind him, and the light from it showed him that, except for the hatrack and table and chairs, the hall was empty. And then, as he stood there, listening to the bumping of his heart, gradually the light faded; the hall grew darker and darker—as if something huge had come up on the porch behind him and stood there, blocking the doorway. He swung round quickly, but there was nothing there. Nothing at all.

He drew a deep breath. It must have been just a cloud passing across the sun. But then the door, all of itself, began to swing shut. And before he could stop it, it closed with a bang. And it was then, as he was pulling frantically at the handle to get out, that Jimmy saw the ghost.

It behaved just as you would expect a ghost to behave. It was a tall, dim, white figure, and it came gliding slowly down the stairs towards him. Jimmy gave a yell, yanked the door open, and tore down the steps.

He didn't stop until he was well down the road. Then he had to get his breath. He sat down on a log. "Boy!" he said. "I've seen a ghost! Golly, was that awful!" Then after a minute, he thought,

"What was so awful about it? He was trying to scare me, like that smart aleck who is always jumping out from behind things. Pretty silly business for a grown-up ghost to be doing."

It always makes you mad when someone deliberately tries to scare you. And as soon as Jimmy got over his fright, he began to get angry. And he got up and started back. "I must get that key, anyway," he thought, for he had left it in the door.

This time, he approached very quietly. He thought he'd just lock the door and go home. But as he tiptoed up the steps, he saw it was still open, and as he reached cautiously for the key, he heard a faint sound. He drew back and peeked around the doorjamb, and there was the ghost.

The ghost was going back upstairs, but he wasn't gliding now, he was doing a sort of dance, and every other step he would bend double and shake with laughter. His thin cackle was the sound Jimmy had heard. Evidently, he was enjoying the

joke he had played. That made Jimmy madder than ever. He stuck his head farther around the doorjamb and yelled "Boo!" at the top of his lungs. The ghost gave a thin shriek and leaped two feet in the air, then collapsed on the stairs.

As soon as Jimmy saw he could scare the ghost even worse than the ghost could scare him, he wasn't afraid any more, and he came right into the hall. The ghost was hanging on to the bannisters and panting. "Oh, my goodness!" he gasped. "Boy, you can't *do* that to me!"

"I did it, didn't I?" said Jimmy. "Now we're even."

"Nothing of the kind," said the ghost crossly. "You seem pretty stupid, even for a boy. Ghosts are supposed to scare people. People aren't supposed to scare ghosts." He got up slowly and glided down and sat on the bottom step. "But look here, boy, this could be pretty serious for me if people got to know about it."

"You mean you don't want me to tell anybody about it?" Jimmy asked.

"Suppose we make a deal," the ghost said, "You keep still about this, and in return I'll—well, let's see. How would you like to know how to vanish?"

"Oh, that would be swell!" Jimmy exclaimed. "But—can you vanish?"

"Sure," said the ghost, and he did. All at once, he just wasn't there. Jimmy was alone in the hall.

But his voice went right on. "It would be pretty handy, wouldn't it?" he said persuasively. "You could get into the movies free whenever you wanted to, and if your aunt called you to do something—when you were in the yard, say— well, she wouldn't be able to find you."

"I don't mind helping Aunt Mary," Jimmy said.

"Hmm. High-minded, eh?" said the ghost. "Well, then—"

"I wish you'd please reappear," Jimmy interrupted. "It makes me feel funny to talk to somebody who isn't there."

"Sorry, I forgot," said the ghost, and there he was again, sitting on the bottom step. Jimmy could see the step, dimly, right through him. "Good trick, eh? Well, if you don't like vanishing, maybe I could teach you to seep through keyholes. Like this." He floated over to the door and went right through the keyhole, the way water goes down the drain. Then he came back the same way.

"That's useful, too," he said. "Getting into locked rooms and so on. You can go anywhere the wind can."

"No," said Jimmy. "There's only one thing you can do to get me to promise not to tell about scaring you. Go live somewhere else. There's Miller's, up the road. Nobody lives there any more."

"That old shack!" said the ghost with a nasty laugh. "Doors and windows half off, roof leaky— no thanks! What do you think it's like in a storm, windows banging, rain dripping on you—I guess not! Peace and quiet, that's really what a ghost wants out of life."

"Well, I don't think it's very fair," Jimmy said, "for you to live in a house that doesn't belong to you, and keep my aunt from renting it."

"Pooh!" said the ghost. "I'm not stopping her from renting it. I don't take up any room, and it's not my fault if people get scared and leave."

"It certainly is!" Jimmy said angrily. "You don't play fair and I'm not going to make any bargain with you. I'm going to tell everybody how I scared you."

"Oh, you mustn't do that!" The ghost seemed quite disturbed, and he vanished and reappeared rapidly several times. "If that got out, every ghost in the country would be in terrible trouble."

So, they argued about it. The ghost said if Jimmy wanted money, he could learn to vanish. Then he could join a circus and get a big salary.

Jimmy said he didn't want to be in a circus, he wanted to go to college and learn to be a doctor. He was firm. And the ghost began to cry.

"But this is my *home,* boy," he said. "Thirty years I've lived here and no trouble to anybody, and now you want to throw me out into the cold world! And for what? A little money! That's pretty heartless." And he sobbed, trying to make Jimmy feel cruel.

Jimmy didn't feel cruel at all, for the ghost had certainly driven plenty of other people out into the cold world. But he didn't really think it would do much good for him to tell anybody that he had scared the ghost. Nobody would believe him, and how could he prove it? So, after a minute, he said, "Well, all right. You teach me to vanish and I won't tell." They settled it that way.

Jimmy didn't say anything to his aunt about what he'd done. But every Saturday, he went to the haunted house for his vanishing lesson. It is really quite easy when you know how. In a couple of weeks he could flicker, and in six weeks the ghost gave him an examination and he got a B plus, which is very good for a human. So, he thanked the ghost and shook hands with him and said, "Well, good-by now. You'll hear from me."

"What do you mean by that?" said the ghost suspiciously. But Jimmy just laughed and ran off home.

That night, at supper, Jimmy's aunt said, "Well, what have you been doing today?"

"I've been learning to vanish."

His aunt smiled and said, "That must be fun."

"Honestly," said Jimmy. "The ghost up at grandfather's taught me."

"I don't think that's very funny," said his aunt. "And will you please not—why, where are you?" she demanded, for he had vanished.

"Here, Aunt Mary," he said as he reappeared.

"Merciful heavens!" she exclaimed, and she pushed back her chair and rubbed her eyes hard. Then she looked at him again.

Well, it took a lot of explaining, and he had to do it twice more before he could persuade her that he really could vanish. She was pretty upset. But, at last, she calmed down and they had a long talk. Jimmy kept his word and didn't tell her that he had scared the ghost, but he said he had a plan, and at last, reluctantly, she agreed to help him.

So, the next day, she went to the old house and started to work. She opened the windows and swept and dusted and aired the bedding, and made as much noise as possible. This disturbed the ghost, and pretty soon he came floating into the room where she was sweeping. She was scared all right. She gave a yell and threw the broom at him. As the broom went right through him and he came nearer, waving his arms and groaning, she shrank back.

And Jimmy, who had been standing there invisible all the time, suddenly appeared and jumped at the ghost with a "Boo!" And the ghost fell over in a dead faint.

As soon as Jimmy's aunt saw that, she wasn't frightened any more. She found some smelling salts and held them under the ghost's nose, and when he came to, she tried to help him into a chair. Of course, she couldn't help him much because her hands went right through him. But, at last, he sat up and said reproachfully to Jimmy, "You broke your word!"

"I promised not to tell about scaring you," said the boy, "but I didn't promise not to scare you again."

And his aunt said, "You really are a ghost, aren't you? I thought you were just stories people made up. Well, excuse me, but I must get on with my work." And she began sweeping and banging around with her broom harder than ever.

The ghost put his hands to his head. "All this noise," he said. "Couldn't you work more quietly, ma'am?"

"Whose house is this, anyway?" she demanded. "If you don't like it, why don't you move out?"

The ghost sneezed violently several times. "Excuse me," he said. "You're raising so much dust. Where's that boy?" he asked suddenly. For Jimmy had vanished again.

"I'm sure I don't know," she replied. "Probably getting ready to scare you again."

"You ought to have better control of him," said the ghost severely. "If he was my boy, I'd take a hairbrush to him."

"You have my permission," she said, and she reached right through the ghost and pulled the chair cushion out from under him and began banging the dust out of it. "What's more," she went on, as he got up and glided wearily to another chair, "Jimmy and I are going to sleep here nights from now on, and I don't think it would be very smart of you to try any tricks."

"Ha, ha," said the ghost nastily. "He who laughs last—"

"Ha, ha, yourself," said Jimmy's voice from close behind him. "And that's me, laughing last."

The ghost muttered and vanished.

Jimmy's aunt put cotton in her ears and slept that night in the best bedroom with the light lit. The ghost screamed for awhile down in the cellar, but nothing happened, so he came upstairs. He thought he would appear to her as two glaring, fiery eyes, which was one of his best tricks, but first he wanted to be sure where Jimmy was. But he couldn't find him. He hunted all over the house, and though he was invisible himself, he got more and more nervous. He kept imagining that, at any moment, Jimmy might jump out at him from some dark corner and scare him into fits. Finally, he got so jittery that he went back to the cellar and hid in the coalbin all night.

The following days were just as bad for the ghost. Several times, he tried to scare Jimmy's aunt while she was working, but she didn't scare worth a cent, and twice Jimmy managed to sneak up on him and appear suddenly with a loud yell, frightening him dreadfully. He was, I suppose, rather timid even for a ghost. He began to look quite haggard. He had several long arguments with Jimmy's aunt, in which he wept and appealed to her sympathy, but she was firm. If he wanted to live there, he would have to pay rent, just like anybody else. There was the abandoned Miller farm two miles up the road. Why didn't he move there?

When the house was all in apple-pie order, Jimmy's aunt went down to the village to see a Mr. and Mrs. Whistler, who were living at the hotel because they couldn't find a house to move into. She told them about the old house, but they said, "No, thank you. We've heard about that house. It's haunted. I'll bet," they said, "*you wouldn't dare spend a night there.*"

She told them that she had spent the last week there, but they evidently didn't believe her. So, she said, "You know my nephew, Jimmy. He's ten years old. I am so sure that the house is not haunted that, if you want to rent it, I will let Jimmy stay there with you every night until you are sure everything is all right."

"Ha!" said Mr. Whistler. "The boy won't do it. He's got more sense."

So, they sent for Jimmy. "Why, I've spent the last week there," he said. "Sure. I'd just as soon."

But the Whistlers still refused.

So, Jimmy's aunt went around and told a lot of the village people about their talk, and everybody made so much fun of the Whistlers for being afraid, when a ten-year-old boy wasn't, that they were ashamed, and said that they would rent it. So, they moved in. Jimmy stayed there for a week, but he saw nothing of the ghost. And then one

day, one of the boys in his grade told him that
somebody had seen a ghost up at the Miller farm.
So, Jimmy knew the ghost had taken his aunt's
advice.

A day or two later, he walked up to the Miller
farm. There was no front door and he walked
right in. There was some groaning and thumping
upstairs, and then, the ghost came floating down.

"Oh, it's you!" he said. "Goodness sakes, boy,
can't you leave me in peace?"

Jimmy said he'd just come up to see how the ghost
was getting along.

"Getting along fine," said the ghost. "From my
point of view it's a very desirable property. Peaceful. Quiet. Nobody playing silly tricks."

"Well," said Jimmy, "I won't bother you if you don't bother the Whistlers. But if you come back there—"

"Don't worry," said the ghost.

So, with the rent money, Jimmy and his aunt had a much easier life. They went to the movies, sometimes twice a week, and Jimmy had all new clothes, and on Thanksgiving, for the first time in his life, Jimmy had a turkey. Once a week, he would go up to the Miller farm to see the ghost, and they got to be very good friends. The ghost even came down to the Thanksgiving dinner, though of course he couldn't eat much. He seemed to enjoy the warmth of the house and he was in very good humor. He taught Jimmy several more tricks. The best one was how to glare with fiery eyes, which was useful later on when Jimmy became a doctor and had to look down people's throats to see if their tonsils ought to come out. He was really a pretty good fellow as ghosts go, and Jimmy's aunt got quite fond of him herself. When the real winter weather began, she even used to worry about him a lot, because of course there was no heat in the Miller place and the doors and windows didn't amount to much and there was hardly any roof. The ghost tried to explain to her that heat and cold didn't bother ghosts at all.

"Maybe not," she said, "but just the same, it can't be very pleasant." And when he accepted their invitation for Christmas dinner, she knitted some warm woolen slippers, and he was so pleased that he broke down and cried. And that made Jimmy's aunt so happy, *she* broke down and cried.

Jimmy didn't cry, but he said, "Aunt Mary, don't you think it would be nice if the ghost came down and lived with us this winter?"

"I would feel very much better about him if he did," she said.

So, the ghost stayed with them that winter, and then he just stayed on, and it must have been a peaceful place for, the last I heard, he was still there.